Ten Minute Tales

In this book you will find
stories from all parts of the
world. You can read about
the Fairy Piper in Ireland,
Ching and Chang in China
and the Seven Little Red
Indian Boys in North
America. Some of the stories
are about animals, some begin
'Once upon a time', but each
has been retold especially for
you to read yourself.

Cover design by Brian Denyer

Ten Minute Tales

Rhoda Power

Illustrations by Elsa Day

Evans Brothers Limited London

First paperback edition 1967
Fourth printing 1973

Originally published in 1942 by
Evans Brothers Limited
Montague House, Russell Square,
London, WC1

© Estate of the late Rhoda Power 1961

Set in 12 on 14 point Intertype
Baskerville and
printed in Great Britain by
Cox & Wyman Ltd., London,
Reading and Fakenham
PB. ISBN 0 237 35040 8   PR 3324
CSD. ISBN 0 237 35228 1

Contents

1   The Fairy Piper

Once upon a time an Irishman called Micky lived in a tiny log cabin with his wife Judy and one little boy. I said 'boy', but really I hardly know how to describe that extraordinary child. He had long, pointed ears. His head was almost bald, with just three little tufts of hair sticking straight up. His legs were as thin as a handle of a whip, and hairy – ugh! And as for his face, it was as wrinkled and wizened as an old man's.

Now Judy and Micky were quite a handsome couple and most people thought it was odd that they had such a peculiar-looking child, but nobody liked to say anything for fear of hurting Judy's feelings. And as for Judy and Micky, they never spoke of the child to anyone. The fact of the matter was the little creature wasn't theirs at all. They'd found it.

Yes, if you please, in the peat-box! Micky had just opened the box to get a piece of peat to throw on the fire when out rolled a baby, simply covered with cobwebs and howling enough to lift the roof. Of course, as soon as Judy heard the cries, in she ran and picked up the little thing and began to cuddle it.

'Now, you put that down!' said Micky. 'Do you hear? Nasty screeching creature! Can't you see what it is? That's a witch child, an imp. The fairies don't want to be bothered with it, so they've left it here. Put it back in the peat-box. Do you hear what I say?'

'Yow-oo – yow-oo!' squawked the baby.

'There, there, there,' said Judy, rocking it in her arms. 'It shan't go back in the peat-box. No, it shan't, then.'

'Yow-oo! yow-oo-ow-oo!' squalled the ugly little thing, kicking its skinny legs and rolling its eyes till they looked as though they'd turn back to front.

'Will you put it back in the peat-box?' said Micky. 'I tell you it will bring us all bad luck.'

'Now, look here, Micky,' said Judy, 'a baby's a baby, whether it's a human child or a fairy. And what decent woman would smother the little soul in a peat-box? Not Judy O'Flanaghan.'

'Oh, woman, woman!' said Micky. 'Will you listen to what I'm telling you? That's not a human soul. That's an imp! Put it down where you found it.'

'Micky O'Flanaghan!' said Judy, 'I wonder you're not ashamed of yourself, talking like that! For all you know, your mother may have taken *you* out of a peat-box. And what would have happened if she'd put you back, pray?'

'Will you cease talking nonsense and do as I ask you?' said Micky.

'No, I will not!' said Judy as she hugged the squalling brat and put it into the only bed in the cabin, and there it lay yelling and rolling its eyes.

When he saw that happen, Micky knew that the goblin baby had come to stay! Judy was too kind to put it back in the peat-box, and Micky was too fond of Judy to make her do what she didn't like.

So the child stayed. They called it Peter because it was found in the peat, and they were as kind to it as though it had been their own little baby.

As time went on, they became more and more certain that it was a witch-child, some sort of fairy. It had such an elfish look. It played such impish tricks, and the funny thing was that although its face became older and older, it hardly *grew* at all. It learned how to eat and to drink, but it was always a *little* creature and it never spoke a word.

It didn't even say 'Dad' or 'Mum'. If it wanted things it snatched them, and if it couldn't get them, it screamed.

At first this annoyed Micky, and he was all for giving the child a good scolding and putting him in the corner, but Judy wouldn't allow that.

'Now, Micky,' said she, 'you were the first person to say that Peter wasn't an ordinary child and so you can't treat him in an ordinary way. If the fairies were to hear us scolding him, they'd never give us any peace. Our only chance of good luck is to be kind to the child.' And she'd go to the cupboard and give the little goblin a cake or a piece of bread and jam to keep him quiet.

Well, life went on from day to day. Peter growing uglier and uglier, but not a bit taller. He fought like a little cat if Judy tried to wash his ears, and if she told him to put on his best clothes and come to church, he ran away and hid the whole Sunday, so that no one could find him.

Micky used to grumble: 'If I find him, you see if I don't punish him this time!' and Judy used to look frightened and say: 'SSh! Micky. The fairies will hear. You can't punish a fairy child. You'll bring us bad luck.'

And so Peter was always sure of his bread and jam or his little cake, and was never punished at all.

One day an old blind piper came to Micky's cabin asking for a glass of milk and a crust of bread. Judy had gone to the market, but Micky was at home and he poured out the milk and cut the bread, saying: 'You're welcome if you'll play a tune on your pipe afterwards.'

The old man drank his milk and ate his bread; then, after he had rested for a while, he put his pipes to his lips and began to play the merriest jig.

Micky was delighted. He beat time with his feet and nodded his head, humming the tune. But the music had the most astonishing effect upon Peter. For the first time in his life, he began to laugh. He chuckled and giggled, holding his sides and slapping his little hairy thighs. Then he began to shuffle his feet and dance.

'What's *that?*' said the old piper.

'That's only the little lad,' said Mick. 'It appears he's musical.'

'Musical are you, my little man,' said the piper. 'Then let's hear what kind of tune you can play. Here you are, catch hold of the pipes.'

The little goblin rushed forward, seized the pipes and put them to his lips. He began to play and *he hadn't played more than two bars* before an extraordinary thing happened.

Everything in the cabin began to dance.

The peat danced out of the peat-box and jigged round the table. The table stood on two legs and jumped up and down. The three-legged stool hopped madly round the room, and as for the old piper he skipped and twirled till he skipped and twirled himself out of the door and far away.

'Put down thim pipes!' shouted Micky in a fright. But Peter only grinned and went on playing. Then the cat danced until her head twisted round and faced her tail. The cow danced into the milk pail and spilt the milk. And Micky's chair danced from underneath him – and down he went with a bump.

'Put down thim pipes!' shouted Micky, making a grab at Peter and missing him.

Peter went on playing and the potatoes danced out of the oven and into the back-yard.

'Will ye put down thim pipes, ye ill-natured scallywag!' shouted Micky, and he seized a wooden spoon which came dancing past, grabbed Peter by the leg, turned him upside down and began to spank him with the spoon. Down fell the pipes with a crash, the music stopped and Peter gave an ear-splitting yell. 'Mamma! Mamma!' he screeched.

'That won't help you,' said Micky, quite forgetting that Peter had never in his life said 'Mamma'. 'You'll do as you're told next time' – and down came the spoon harder and faster than ever.

'Mamma!' screamed Peter with a yell that was loud enough to lift off the roof.

And – well – as a matter of fact it did lift off the roof! Yes, really! Micky's thatched roof rose in the air and floated away and down through the hole came an old woman riding on a broomstick. Micky had only just time to notice that she and Peter were as like as two peas, when she gave him a bump with the broomstick which sent him sprawling.

'Mamma!' screeched Peter.

'You naughty little goblin,' cried the old woman, seizing Peter by the seat of his breeches and flinging him across the broomstick. 'What do you mean by calling me when I'm so busy? Wait till I get you home, and off you'll go to the imps' school to learn manners.'

Still scolding, she rose in the air, and when Micky looked up he saw her high above the trees flying like the wind, with Peter still sprawling across her broomstick.

As for Micky, well, he and Judy never saw Peter again, and ever afterwards they lived in a house without a roof. They were never rich enough to mend it, poor things.

2 The Old Woman and the Little Fir Tree

Once upon a time there was a little old woman who knew all about magic. She lived in a forest, and every day she used to listen to what the trees were saying. Trees talk, you know, not as you and I do, but in their own language – a whispering of leaves and a little crackling of branches. And because the old woman knew all about magic, she understood what they were saying. Sometimes, if she heard a tree wishing for something, she nodded her head, wiggle-waggle, wiggle-waggle; then, because she knew magic, the wish came true.

One day she heard a little fir tree talking to its mother. The little tree had rather a cross voice; it was grumbling.

'I hate being myself,' said the little fir tree. 'Look at these needles instead of pretty leaves. Why can't I be like the silver birch? Its leaves sparkle in the sun and glisten in the rain. I'm ugly. I hate being myself.'

'Now that's silly,' said its mother. She was a tall, dark-needled fir tree, very handsome, and she looked down at the little one in a kind, protecting way.

'You know, my dear, we can't have everything in the world, and if we take the trouble to think about it, we soon find that we each have some good things ourselves.'

The little fir tree looked sulky. 'I haven't got any good things,' it said; 'the birch tree has. She has silver leaves which sparkle in the sun and glisten in the rain.'

'Now just think a little,' said its mother rustling her needles and looking down at her cross child. 'In the winter when the cold winds come, one by one the poor birch tree will lose all its leaves. Its branches will be bare and cold. The wind won't tear off your needles – they will stay green all the winter.'

But still the little fir tree drooped and looked cross. 'I shall never be happy,' it said, 'until I have silver leaves that sparkle in the sun and glisten in the rain.'

The old woman was listening. She nodded her head, wiggle-waggle, wiggle-waggle, and because she knew magic the wish came true.

The little fir tree's needles fell to the ground and it was covered with tiny silver leaves like the birch tree.

How proud it was! It swayed this way and that, stretching its branches and making all the leaves quiver. 'Look,' it said, 'look, Mother! All my leaves sparkle in the sun and glisten in the rain.' A few mornings later there was a rustling in the forest, and an old grey goat came by with a little white kid.

'Ma-a-a, Ma-a-a, I'm hungry,' said the kid.

'Now, now, don't you run off, my darling,' said the goat. 'There's plenty to eat. Why! Look at this little tree with the fresh young leaves. Those will be very good for you.'

And then and there the old grey goat and the little white kid went up to the fir tree and began to tear off its new leaves.

'Crunch, crunch, crunch,' went the old grey goat, and 'nibble, nibble, nibble,' went the little white kid.

And with the crunching and the nibbling all the little fir tree's new leaves were eaten up, and it was left with bare brown branches.

It looked very strange and ugly, and it felt very cold. It was lonely too, for the birds were afraid of it and wouldn't come and perch on its branches.

You can imagine how thankful it was when the sun shone and fresh showers of rain began to fall, and all its own little green needles began to sprout once more. Within a year the fir tree was quite itself again, and its mother looked down upon it fondly and whispered loving words.

But strangely enough, as the weeks passed, the baby fir tree forgot how pleased it had been when its needles had begun to grow again, and once more it began to droop and look unhappy. Autumn had come, and the leaves of every tree except the fir were scarlet or gold, and a carpet of golden leaves lay on the ground.

The little fir drooped with discontent.

'Oh, dear!' it said, 'how I wish I had golden leaves. Look at the chestnut tree. It's dressed all in gold. I hate my horrid green needles.'

'Now, now!' said the old fir tree, 'don't be a silly, discontented little thing. Don't you see, every time the wind comes it tears off those leaves and flings them on the ground and people tramp on them. Your green needles can never come to harm.'

'It's all very well to talk like that,' said the little fir tree. 'I'm ugly and you know it. Oh, how I hate being myself. Why can't I have golden leaves?'

'You wouldn't have them for long,' answered its mother. 'I told you, the wind would soon carry them off.'

'It wouldn't carry them off if they were solid gold, real gold,' said the fir tree. 'If only I had solid gold leaves, how lovely I should look!'

The little old woman happened to be passing at that moment. She nodded her head, wiggle-waggle, wiggle-waggle, and because she knew magic the wish came true. Immediately all the little green needles fell off the fir tree and it was covered with real gold leaves.

'Ha, ha!' laughed the tree. 'Now I'm grand. Look at me! Aha! I'm finer than any tree in the forest. I shall sparkle in the sun, shine in the rain, and the wind can't hurt me.'

The foolish little thing stood up very straight and stiff, showing its solid gold leaves to all the other trees in the forest, and proudly trying to shake its branches. But it could hardly move. The golden leaves were very heavy, and soon the little fir tree's branches bent to the ground with the weight of the gold. It couldn't sway or bow when the wind passed through the forest, and it soon grew tired, but still it held its head high and said: 'Look at me! I'm finer than any other tree.'

Now you know, don't you, that there are greedy people in the world, and people who want to take things away from others who have more than themselves? One day a greedy man happened to be walking through the forest with a wheelbarrow, and he saw the little fir tree with the golden leaves.

His eyes gleamed. 'Gold!' he whispered. 'Real gold! If I cut off these leaves I shall be richer than anyone else in the land.'

He looked around. There was nobody about. He took a penknife out of his pocket and began to cut off the golden leaves. In his haste he didn't care how he hacked and chopped at the little fir tree's twigs and branches. He sawed, he cut, he broke and he twisted, and then he went away with his wheelbarrow full of gold leaves, and he left behind a poor little tree, almost dead, with its branches all broken.

For months the poor little thing was miserable and sore. Sadly it struggled to live, doing its best to put forth tiny shoots and to heal its bruised, torn bark. By degrees, the soft air and the sunshine helped it to grow stronger, and the next time that the old woman was passing she heard the little fir tree whispering: 'I never want to be anything but myself.'

And the old mother fir answered: 'Well, well, the world

will be a happier place when we all stop wanting what other people have.'

Then the little old woman nodded her head, wiggle-waggle. 'There's magic in that,' she said. And *she* knew.

Do *you* know what she meant?

3   The Seven Supperless Boys

Once upon a time seven Red Indian boys lived with their mother in the heart of a deep forest in North America.

The eldest was tall and well-grown, with long black hair and shining brown eyes, and his name was Sharp-Arrow. Although he was so big and strong, Sharp-Arrow was still a child like his six little brothers, and so he spent most of his time with them. And, like your days, their days were spent eating, sleeping, dressing, playing and doing lessons.

For Sharp-Arrow and his brothers, lessons were the most important. Without lessons they wouldn't have been able to eat, and without lessons they wouldn't have slept snugly and peacefully in their wigwam, nor played undisturbed in the forest. If they hadn't learnt their lessons they wouldn't have had any clothes to wear or shoes to put on their feet. You see, all their lessons were in some way or other connected with hunting. Hunting brought them skins for clothing, food to eat, and rugs to cover them when they slept. Hunting kept the wild beasts away from the wigwam, so that the seven boys could lie down in peace at night or play undisturbed by day.

Every day all the brothers except the youngest went into the forest to learn their lessons. They walked with their eyes fixed to the ground, looking for the tracks of the wild beasts. They knew when the old grizzly bear had passed that way. They could trace the fox to his den, follow the deer and hunt the marten and the beaver. From the animals' skins their mother made shirts and leggings. From the dried sinews she made thread to sew with, and from the bones she made needles and spoons.

When the children had done well at the hunt their mother would say: 'Good boys! You're worthy of your names.' And the boys would glow with pride, for all except the youngest had hunting names. There was Sharp-Arrow, who never missed his mark, White-Hawk, who swooped down upon his prey like a fierce wild bird, and Angry-Cub, who never cried like an ordinary child, but growled like a little bear. There was Quick-I-Spy, who had sharp eyes, Master-Fleetly-Run, who was swift on foot, and Laughing-Boy, who always chuckled when he had a good hunting.

The seventh who was still almost a papoose – that is, a baby – hadn't a hunting name at all. He was called Little-

Cuddly-One, and he never did any lessons, but lay in the wigwam in a cradle made of birch-bark lined with moss, and only tumbled out of it when he heard his brothers come back from their hunting and begin to play. Then he waddled towards them on his small fat legs and joined in the games as best he could.

Every day when the older boys came back from their lessons in the forest they were very hungry. Usually they had been hunting all day, or tracking or learning how to make pens into which they could drive the animals, or weaving snares to catch them. And not a bite or sup did they have until they reached home. Then into the wigwam they would tumble, and shout for a meal. Sometimes they had a delicious stew or a thick soup with lumps of meat in it. Sometimes they had deer's flesh, sometimes little yellow cakes of maize spread with honey. Even in the winter, when it was not easy to provide food, their mother always had something for them. And when they had finished they would jump up, pick Little-Cuddly-One out of the cradle and carry him into the forest to say a prayer.

It may seem a strange prayer to you, but to the little Red Indians it was quite familiar. Every night they would go behind the forest, stand on a green hill, look up at the stars and sing the Star-Song:

'Seven little hunters gazing at the sky,
Sharp-Arrow, White Hawk and Quick-I-Spy!
Laughing-Boy and Angry-Cub, Master-Fleetly-Run
And last of all the baby, Little-Cuddly-One!

Now the day is over, everything is dark;
Seven little hunters are singing to you, hark!
Twinkle till the morning, don't put out your light,
And keep the little hunters safe and sound tonight.'

And the stars would shine more brightly than ever and
would answer in twinkling, star-like voices which seemed to
laugh:

'Silly little children, hunting all the day
Must be very tiring! Why not run away?
Twinkling must be better. Won't you come and try?
Jump! The stars will catch you, jump into the sky.'

But the boys always shook their heads and, catching up
Little-Cuddly-One, they would run home as fast as they
could. They didn't want to be stars. They much preferred
hunting. They thought it would be rather cold and dull,
twinkling all night in the sky, and so whenever the stars
called down their invitation the boys shook their heads and
ran home.

Well, time passed and although the boys grew more skil-
ful with bows, arrows and canoes, their hunting was not
always quite so successful as it ought to have been. Perhaps
the wild beasts were growing more careful, or they were
scarce. Anyhow, the season was bad and the boys did not
bring home very much. They used to start earlier and stay
out much later, but this only meant that they came home
much hungrier than before, and into the wigwam they

would bound and shout for a meal. At first their mother managed to have something in the pot – in any case, enough to go round; but naturally when hunting was bad there came a time when meals were not very good either.

The boys were hungry. And when people are hungry they are not always very good tempered, and they do and say things which they would never do and say if they were feeling perfectly well and happy. The boys took to grumbling at meal-time. Angry-Cub was the worst. He used to snarl like a little animal and snatch more than his share. Master-Fleetly-Run always got back to the wigwam before the others, and then if his mother did not keep a sharp look-out he would dip into the pot. White-Hawk would swoop down on the food, like his namesake, and run off with a big bit before anyone could stop him. Even Laughing Boy began to look cross. In fact the only one who was amiable was Little-Cuddly-One, and he just lay in his birch-bark cradle and sucked his thumb.

Then one day a most unfortunate thing happened. Quick-I-Spy and Sharp-Arrow discovered their mother's store cupboard. It was a basket hidden under the ground with a long mound of earth on the top of it. There was some delicious yellow corn in it. Before anyone could say 'Tomahawk!' the boys had thrown it into the pot and had begun to cook it. For the first time in several weeks they had a good meal, and they ran out to sing the Star-Song, leaving their mother in the wigwam shaking her head and saying, 'Yes! And what are you going to eat tomorrow?'

The next day the six little hunters went off as usual, but

they had no luck at all. They did not even catch a rabbit. Most of them dawdled home, feeling slightly ashamed. Angry-Cub was grousing, and Quick-I-Spy looking into every corner with his bright eyes. Presently Sharp-Arrow said 'Look!' White-Hawk and Master-Fleetly-Run, who had hurried on ahead of the others, were returning and their faces were angry.

'There's no supper!' they cried.

No supper! The others looked blank.

'Isn't there even soup?' asked Laughing-Boy.

'Not a drop! We've looked everywhere,' said White-Hawk, 'and there's no one in the wigwam but Little-Cuddly-One and he's sucking his thumb.'

The others began to run! Sure enough there was no one but the papoose in the wigwam and not a scrap of supper. The pot was upside down on the hearth and beside it the empty store basket.

The boys sat down and waited. They were sure their mother would come back with something to eat, and they looked longingly at the empty pot. Gradually it grew darker and at last, when it was almost bedtime, their mother came in.

'Now then, boys!' she said, 'It's time for the Star-Song. Take Little-Cuddly-One and be off.'

'But – but – we haven't had supper,' said Laughing-Boy, and he smiled a coaxing smile at his mother.

'No! We haven't had supper,' growled Angry-Cub.

'I seem to remember that you had today's supper yesterday,' said their mother.

'But we're hungry!' cried White-Hawk.

'You had two suppers last night,' said their mother. 'You must wait till tomorrow! Now be off to your Star-Song.' And she took Little-Cuddly-One out of his cradle and put him in Sharp-Arrow's arms, and gently pushed all seven boys out of the wigwam.

The hungry little hunters slowly made their way to the clearing behind the forest and climbed the green hill. Their faces were grumpy and they felt very empty. They were so hungry that they thought they would never be able to sing.

They looked up. The stars seemed very near and very bright. They twinkled mockingly and down from the sky in crisp starry voices came the song:

'Hungry little hunters, gazing at the sky,
Sharp-Arrow, White-Hawk and Quick-I-Spy!
Laughing-Boy and Angry-Cub, Master-Fleetly-Run,
Hungry, aren't you hungry, Little-Cuddly-One?

'Silly little hunters, hungry all the day,
Why not leave the wigwam? Why not run away?
Jump up here and twinkle. Won't you come and try?
Jump! The stars will catch you, jump into the sky.'

The boys looked at each other and then at the sky. The stars seemed nearer than ever tonight. They seemed to beckon and their voices sounded like the tinkling of bells.

'Stars are never hungry, hungry all the day!
Won't you join the stars, then? Hunters, run away!
Come up here and twinkle! Hunters, won't you try?
Jump! The stars will catch you, jump into the sky.'

Then Sharp-Arrow took Little-Cuddly-One in his arms
and looked at his brothers. He was trembling, but his voice
was very clear. 'One, two, three,' he cried.

'Away,' shouted the others.

They sprang into the air. Up, up, up, they floated until
they reached the sky; and if you look out of the window on
a dark night you can still see the little supperless hunters
gazing down at the world – seven twinkling stars.

There is one big bright one. That's Sharp-Arrow. There
are five which are smaller and not so bright. Those are his
brothers. And if you look carefully, you'll see one little tiny
star that hardly shows. He's Little-Cuddly-One. He never
wanted to jump and he sometimes cries for that birch-bark
cradle in the old wigwam, and so his light is rather dim.

That is really the end of the story, but there is something
else which you may like to know. In our part of the world,
we call that group of stars the Pleiades, a name which the
Greeks gave to them long ago; but they told quite a different
story.

4   The Wishing-Skin

Once upon a time there was a woodcutter whose name was
Rudolf. He was very poor, and he lived with his wife in a
little hut made of split logs, in the middle of a deep forest.

The forest was so thick that people scarcely ever passed
Rudolf's hut. But the woodcutter wasn't lonely. When he
was at home he sat by the fire, talking to his wife; and when
he was in the woods, he made friends with the birds and the
animals. The furry beasts and the little feathered folk used to
watch him out of their bright eyes and come quite close to
his feet without being afraid. Then Rudolf would look at
them and say: 'Good morning, little comrades! I'd rather
have friends like you than all the riches in the world.'

One day the king came hunting in the woods, looking for
wild deer. Princes and princesses came with him, and lords

and ladies too. They came once. They came twice. They came three times. And they liked it so much that after that they came nearly every day.

Their clothes were of velvet edged with fur. They rode fine horses with little silver bells round their necks, and they had servants dressed in green and gold who brought baskets of food for them to eat when they were hungry, and flasks of sparkling wine to drink when they were thirsty.

Sometimes they stopped at Rudolf's little hut and peeped in and laughed, saying: 'See the funny old table with no fine linen! Look, he hasn't any chairs! How quaint! How old-fashioned!' and they would sit on Rudolf's three-legged stools and say: 'Ooh, how hard! He must wear out his breeches without a velvet cushion.' And when they saw the darns and patches in Rudolf's breeches, they laughed and said: 'Ha! ha! We were right.' When Rudolf heard this he was ashamed of his poor hut and his ugly, darned breeches, and little by little he began to grow discontented.

He began to wonder why he should be poor and they rich, and he went about his work with such a long face that the birds were afraid of him, and he heaved such deep, grumbling sighs that all the little beasts scuttled into the woods in a fright – at least, all save the rabbit.

The rabbit sat back on his haunches, flopped his ears and wobbled his nose. 'Why, what's the matter with you, Rudolf?'

'Nothing,' said Rudolf, grumpily. 'I wish I were rich. That's all.'

'Pah,' said the rabbit. 'What's the good of wishing without the wishing-skin? Spare your breath, Rudolf.'

Rudolf straightened his back and put down his hatchet. 'Eh?' said he. 'Wishing-skin, did you say? And what may that be, Bunny?'

The rabbit whisked round with a flicker of his white tail. 'Half a minute,' he said, 'I'll show you,' and he skipped behind a bush, returning almost at once with a thin, cobwebby skin. 'There, that's the wishing-skin. But don't tell anyone you've seen it. It belongs to the fairies, and they always hide it. They're afraid of its being stolen. You see it's very valuable. It's made of wishes.'

Rudolf looked at the rabbit out of the corner of his eye, cunningly. 'Bunny,' said he, 'suppose I try it on? I'd like to know what it's like to wear a wishing-skin.'

The rabbit looked doubtful.

'Well,' said he, after a pause, 'I don't know whether I ought to let you do that. It's not mine, and, you know, if you were to wish by accident after you had put it on, the fairies would know and I should get into trouble. You see, whenever you wish, the skin gets a little smaller, because one wish is gone. If you're wearing the wishing-skin all your wishes come true.'

Rudolf's hands began to shake, so he put them behind his back. 'Don't be so silly, Bunny,' said he. 'As if I should get you into trouble. Let me try it on. Come on! See, I've taken off my coat.'

He put his coat on the ground and then – well, then, I'm afraid, he did rather a mean thing. He clapped his hands suddenly so that the rabbit jumped backwards in a fright and before the startled little creature could do anything, Rudolf had put on the wishing-skin and was grinning from ear to ear.

'Ha, ha, ha!' he laughed. 'I wish it would stick to me and become a part of me.'

'Oh! Oh!' cried the rabbit. 'Give it back! What will the fairies say? You've made it smaller already.' He stamped with his hind legs on the ground and his eyes looked as though they were going to pop out of his head. 'Do you hear me? Give it back!'

'How can I?' grinned Rudolf. 'It's a part of me, stupid!'

'Oh!' wailed the rabbit. 'Give it back!' And he cried so bitterly that Rudolf was a little ashamed, and somehow, because he was ashamed he grew angry.

'Will you be quiet?' said he. 'I wish you were at the other end of the earth, I do, with your "Give it backs". I —' He stopped and rubbed his eyes. The rabbit had disappeared.

'Why! What?' began Rudolf. Then he remembered. He had wished the rabbit at the other end of the earth, and the wishing-skin had sent it there.

'Hurrah!' shouted Rudolf, capering about. 'Hurrah! Now I can get whatever I want.' And he picked up his coat and ran back to his hut as hard as he could. When he reached the door, he thought for a few minutes, then he walked in and sat down by the fire. 'Wife,' said he, 'have you got a good supper – chicken and sauce and sausages?'

His wife stared at him, half afraid. 'Have you gone mad,

Rudolf?' she asked. 'Chicken, sauce, sausages! Here's your good bread and honey.'

'Pooh!' said Rudolf. 'I wish for chicken, sauce and sausages! I wish for wine! I wish for a nice table spread with fine linen, with silver spoons and golden plates! I wish for chairs and velvet cushions!'

'Stop! Stop!' cried his wife, falling into one of the new chairs, for the wishes were coming true every minute. 'How? — What? — Why? —'

'The wishing-skin, my dear,' said her husband. And then he told her all about it.

You should have seen that woman's face. It grew quite red, and the eyes goggled! You ought to have heard what she said. But if you had heard that, well, you wouldn't have heard very much, because she was almost too astonished to speak. But when she recovered from her amazement, she wouldn't give her husband any peace. She simply made him wish all night. It was 'Wish for this!' 'Wish for that!' 'Now wish for fine clothes,' and they found themselves beautifully dressed. 'Now wish for six bags of gold,' and on the table there were six bags of golden coins. 'Now wish for a fine house, and a garden full of flowers and lots and lots of servants.' And instead of the little wooden hut at the edge of the forest, a fine house appeared with a garden full of flowers and servants everywhere! Cooks in the kitchen, butlers in the pantry, maids in the bedrooms, and footmen with powdered wigs and silk stockings standing on each side of every stair (and there were three flights of stairs).

But you know, it was all very well to have such riches –

but to tell you the truth, a dreadful thing was happening! Rudolf's wife was so busy making him wish, that she didn't notice that her husband was shrinking. Yes! Rudolf was getting smaller.

You see how it was happening, don't you?

Of course you do! Don't you remember? Rudolf had wished the skin to become a part of himself. Each time he wished it became smaller, so of course he became smaller too.

Poor old Rudolf! He didn't like it at all. He was afraid to wish himself bigger, because then he might burst out of the wishing-skin and it would be of no more use. The difficulty was that his wife simply wouldn't be satisfied. She went on making him wish, until at last she wished that he was a king and she was a queen in the most beautiful palace in the land.

But, oh dear, it wasn't very nice for Rudolf. You see, by this time he had become so small that he had to have his meals, not *at* the table, but *on* the table. He had a special little throne, like a doll's chair, and a special little table made by the carpenter. They were put on the big table in the banqueting hall and there the little king had his meals. This was rather undignified for a king, don't you think? I am afraid everybody who came into the banqueting hall thought so too, even the servants. They couldn't help being amused when they had to hand the dishes and pour out tiny glasses of wine for the queer little object sitting on the table. And all the grand lords and ladies who came to visit the new king and queen felt exactly the same. They did their best to be polite, but the little king sitting on the table seemed such a joke that they couldn't help playing with him as though he were a toy. And that was dreadful, because Rudolf still had the feelings of a grown-up man, although he was so small.

After a time something happened which was worse still. Rudolf's wife began to despise him. She was offended and angry when people laughed at him because she thought they were laughing at her for having such a silly little husband. She tried to prevent Rudolf from coming into the banqueting hall and hurried him out of the way whenever she was expecting an important visitor. At last, she hid him from sight. She built him a tiny little doll's house in the garden and never went to see him except when she wanted him to wish for something.

You can imagine how lonely he was, can't you? Poor little king! He used to get up in the morning and put on his crown and look out of the window, wondering how much smaller he was going to get and whether he would soon disappear altogether.

Then, one day when he was looking out of the window, a woodcutter chanced to walk by. He had a hatchet in his hand and a load of wood on his shoulders, and he walked along the path past the doll's house whistling a tune and looking ever so happy.

Rudolf saw him and sighed deeply. 'Oh!' he cried, 'how I envy that happy man. I wish I could forget all this and be a woodcutter with my wife and cottage again!'

A cold wind suddenly blew in his face. He looked up and –

well, if you had peeped into the forest at that moment you would have seen Rudolf picking up a bundle of faggots – and at his feet a little brown rabbit. And the rabbit – yes, I think the rabbit would have been a little bit out of breath.

5   The Gnome who wanted a Lodging

Once upon a time, long, long ago, there was a village which nestled at the foot of some high mountains. The people who lived there were farmers. They had fat cattle which grazed in the green pastures, and sheep and goats which wandered about the hillside. They were healthy happy people, who lived in peace, sheltered by the old mountains which towered above their little village like giants.

Sometimes these mountains were tipped with golden sunshine. Sometimes the moon made them silver, and sometimes their tops were almost hidden by angry clouds. The villagers said that deep, deep under them there was a world of gold and sparkling jewels where the gnomes lived. These little men with long grey beards and tiny brown hands were as busy as bees under the ground, storing up the treasures of the earth, chipping jewels out of the rocks and polishing them till they shone like gleaming lamps.

People who climbed up the mountains by day sometimes heard the tap-tap-tap of their hammers, but they never saw the gnomes till the sun had set. Then, a late shepherd returning to the village, or the little goatherds driving their animals home, sometimes caught sight of a grey beard and a pointed red hat behind a rock. And once or twice in the winter, when the farmers were coming home with their lanterns lit and big felt snow boots on their feet, they had heard a rumbling sound on the mountainside and seen a long procession of little old men with red hats on their heads and heavy sacks on their backs. Nobody spoke to the gnomes, because, for some reason, they were a little afraid of them, and they used to say: 'If we don't interfere with the little folk, they won't interfere with us.'

One day, when the air was very heavy and great clouds hid the tops of the mountains, the gnomes seemed very busy underground. Their tapping was very loud and some of the loose stones on the mountainside began to roll down into the village. The villagers came out of their houses and looked up at the sky. Dark, angry clouds hung low in the air, in the distance lightning flashed, and there was a far-off rumble of thunder.

'We had better bring the cattle home,' said the farmers. 'There'll be a storm here very soon. Run, boys, to the mountain and collect the sheep and the goats.'

As the air grew hotter and the sky darker, the villagers

hurried to bring their animals to safety. They were only just in time. No sooner was the last goat under cover than the storm burst. Thunder rolled and echoed from hill to hill. Streaks of lightning flashed across the sky and the rain poured down in sheets.

'Have you ever seen such a storm?' said the villagers. 'What a mercy the cattle are safe. It's good to be dry and comfortable indoors. To be out on a night like this would be terrible.' And they lit their lamps and listened cosily to the kettles humming on the fire. They were safe and warm, with their curtains drawn and the storm raging outside.

But somebody wasn't safe and warm. Somebody was out in the rain, slipping in the mud, soaked to the skin and shivering. It was a little gnome. He had been a long journey and he had lost his way, and now the storm was raging and there he was, out in the cold, instead of being safe underground. The colour from his scarlet cap was running all down his face in red streaks. One of his long pointed shoes had gone, and the other was torn so that his toes came poking through the end. He still carried a bag on his shoulder, but it was heavier than ever because it was so wet. With bent shoulders and shivering body, the poor little fellow stumbled along slithering over the slippery mud, wading through the water until at last he came to the first cottage in the village.

With a sigh of relief the little man put his sack on the step and tapped at the door. 'Who's there?' asked the owner of the house, and a small tired voice answered:

'Undo the lock!
Did you hear me knock?
A little gnome is calling
While the rain is falling;
He's much too old
To be left in the cold!'

There was a whispered conversation inside, but the door didn't open. Somebody came and shouted through the keyhole: 'You go back to the mountain! How do we know you won't do us harm? Go to your mountain!'

The rain poured down in torrents and the gnome sighed. He wrung the water out of his long grey beard, picked up his bundle and set out again. On he went, slithering and stumbling until he came to the next cottage. There was a hole in the blind and he peeped through. It looked warm and cosy inside. There was a kettle on the fire and a cat sleeping in front of it and two little boys and their parents drinking hot soup out of wooden bowls. The little gnome tapped on the window.

'Undo the lock!
Did you hear me knock?'

'Hallo!' said the mistress of the house. 'Who's that?' One of the children slid off his chair and ran to the door. 'Leave that door alone,' said his father. 'Do you want a gust of wind to blow out the lamp and set the place on fire? Sit down.' He went to the window and looked under the blind. 'Who's there and what do you want?' he asked.

The gnome clambered up to the window-sill. There were tears in his eyes and they rolled down his cheeks among the raindrops, but his face was so wet and woebegone that you couldn't tell which was rain and which were tears. He tapped again.

> 'A little gnome is calling
> While the rain is falling!
> He's much too old
> To be left in the cold!'

'He's old enough to know better than to be late on a night like this,' said the farmer. 'Be off to the mountain. We've no room for drowned rats here.' And he dropped the blind.

Outside the wind blew more strongly than ever and the poor gnome could scarcely keep his feet, but he struggled on to the third cottage and, knocking at the door, cried through the keyhole:

> 'The raindrops are falling
> Helter skelter!
> A poor gnome is calling.
> Give him shelter.'

'A gnome!' shouted a voice. 'Get away from here at once. Your place is underground! What are you doing amongst honest folk at this time of night?'

'Did you hear me knock?
Undo the lock!'

sobbed the poor little gnome, but the door never opened and he went on to the next house.

By this time he was shivering with cold and scarcely able to walk, but no one had pity on him. From house to house he struggled. If the owners opened the doors, they only shut them again; but more often the door was never opened at all, only a cross voice told the gnome to get back to the mountain. By the time he came to the last house, a miserable little hut with no window and a very rickety door, the gnome was so tired that he hadn't the strength to knock. He fell in a little soaked heap on the ground and cried 'Help!'

'Listen,' said a gentle voice in the hut. 'Someone is crying. Oh, husband! Somebody's out on a night like this.'

'Then he won't be out for long,' said a man's voice. 'Give me the lantern. I'll find him and fetch him in!'

The door opened and an old shepherd came to the step and stumbled over the little creature lying on the ground. 'Bless me, wife!' said he. 'Here's a gnome. He's been caught in the rain and he's all but drowned. Come along, little sir. Here's a fire! We're all together. Sheep and lambs and me and my missis. Warm as toast we are. Come in!' And he picked up the little creature and began to dry him in front of the fire.

'You poor little gentleman,' said the wife. 'You're nearly famished with the cold. Try a sup of this.' She gave him her bowl of soup and dipped a crust of bread in it.

Gradually the gnome began to revive and when he was dry and warm again he thanked the old couple warmly, shouldered his bundle and said he must set off. 'On a night like this!' said the old man and his wife in one breath. 'But you mustn't think of it. Stay with us, Mr Gnome. We have only a bed of straw to offer you and a share of our poor breakfast, but you're welcome.'

But the gnome only said:

> 'Kindly folk, I cannot stop,
> For I have work on the mountain-top.'

And before the old people could speak again, he had opened the door and disappeared.

All night the storm raged and they wondered what had happened to their little visitor, but soon to their fear for his safety was added a fear for their own. Torrents of rain poured down and, as the wind roared, great trees were uprooted and bushes tossed from one place to another. Soon water began to flood all through the valley.

The old shepherd and his wife rushed to the door of their hut wailing. 'We shall drown. We shall drown.'

Then suddenly they noticed that something was dancing and leaping on an enormous tree trunk which was being swept along by the water. It was the little gnome. Small as he was, he was steering it with a branch of a fir tree. And as it came near to the shepherd's hut, the great trunk stood still. The water was stemmed. It divided into two streams, one on each side of the rock, and did not even splash the little hut.

The old couple fell down on their knees, but when they looked up, the gnome has disappeared. Only their little hut remained with a tree trunk on one side of it and a broad stream of water in front and behind.

When the storm was over, they made themselves a boat and they rowed with their sheep and lambs to the next valley, where they lived to a ripe old age, and many a time they told the story of a little gnome who had paid for his lodgings by saving the hut which had sheltered him.

6 Why the Owl only comes out at Night

Once upon a time, thousands and thousands of years ago, the birds lived in a world of their own, where there were neither men, nor women nor children. It was a pleasant world and the birds were very comfortable and happy. Although there was no one to scatter crumbs, there was plenty to eat. There were berries on many of the trees, little green insects which were a great delicacy, and common worms for those who didn't like either insects or berries. There was no difficulty about making homes either, for there was plenty of space. There were trees with forked branches, hedges where a nest could be comfortably hidden among the leaves and twigs, delightful little nooks and crannies in the moss, and nice cosy spots among the reeds for the water-fowl. Altogether the birds were exceedingly comfortable and they lived happy contented lives, until one day something happened – snow fell!

Yes, little white flakes came tumbling down from the sky, the ponds where the birds used to drink were frozen, and the world grew chilly and cold.

I suppose you think that this ought not to have made any difference to the birds, but you see, this was the first time that they had ever seen winter. In the world of the birds it had always been spring or summer. Everything had been warm and comfortable. They had no trouble in finding food and water. They had never been cold. Even the rain had seemed sweet and fresh and warm. The birds were frightened.

They sat shivering on the branches of the trees, or tucked their heads under their wings, and cowered in any sheltered corner that they could find. But still the snow fell, and by and by the earth was covered with a white carpet. Pools and ponds were sheets of ice. Frost spoilt all the berries and the poor little birds could scarcely find anything to eat. They were miserable – miserable because they were cold and hungry, and they had never been cold and hungry before.

For some time they stayed where they were, scarcely daring to move, until an old stork who had been standing on one leg for three days suddenly stretched himself, put both legs on the ground and began to pick his way carefully across the snow. Presently he raised his head, snapped his beak together angrily two or three times and squawked: 'Come! Come! Come! This won't do.'

The birds peered at him anxiously from their perches and

nervously ruffled their feathers. The stork clapped his beak again.

'Do you hear?' he said. 'This won't do, I say. We can't stay here shivering for ever. We must call a meeting and settle something. Cock, sound the clarion! Let all the birds fall in.'

The cock, who was shivering in a corner beside a fallen tree, gave the ghost of a crow. Nobody took any notice.

'Louder,' said the stork.

'Cock-a-doodle-do,' gasped the cock.

'Louder still,' shouted the stork, and at last the cock gave a loud crow! The effect was magical. The birds were used to coming at once when a meeting was called, and in a few minutes the sky was black with wings. The eagle swooped down from the mountains. The pelican came from the pool, the penguin waddled up from the seashore like a tired old man. There was a sea-gull, a thrush, a blackbird, a magpie, a starling, a blue-tit, a chaffinch and ever so many more. Last, and very nearly least, came the little wren, so small that it could scarcely be seen.

At first the birds did not know where they were to meet, for the world looked so different now that it was covered with snow; but when they saw the stork, who was always president of the meetings, they settled around him in a circle and waited.

'Birds,' said the stork, 'I have called a meeting because something must be done to keep us warm. If anyone has a good idea, let him speak.'

The birds began to twitter together, but nobody seemed

to have any ideas. There was a dead silence. Suddenly the hen gave a cackle. 'Tee-tah-tuk,' said she.

'I beg your pardon?' said the stork, leaning forward politely.

'Tarra-wa-tuk!' said the hen, shyly standing first on one leg and then on the other. 'Tuk-tuk-tuk! Give-us-heat! Tuk-tuk-tuk! Give-us-heat.'

'Precisely,' said the stork politely. 'We have met together for that reason! Do you suggest *how* we shall get heat?'

The hen was abashed. 'Twork,' said she, and refused to take any further part in the conversation, and once again there was silence.

At last the eagle raised its head. 'I've been thinking,' it said. 'We must light a bonfire. If we keep it burning night and day, we shall be warm again.'

'Caw-caw,' cried the rook. 'How shall we get fire?'

'From the sun,' said the lark, who used to fly so high when she was singing that she knew all about the heat of the sun.

'An excellent idea!' said the stork solemnly. 'Now, will some kind friend volunteer to fly up to the sun and bring down some fire? Who will be kind enough to do that?'

'Who-oo? Who-oo?' asked the owl, but nobody answered. All the birds were looking up at the sky and wondering who would have the courage to fly so very high.

'Well?' said the stork anxiously. Once again there was silence. Each bird seemed to be waiting for his neighbours to volunteer, and when the silence was broken they all began to make excuses at once, until the stork angrily snapped his beak and called for order.

'When you have quite finished quarrelling,' he said, 'I shall be glad to know who will go up to the sun and borrow some fire!'

'Who-oo? Who-oo?' asked the owl again.

'If you please, sir,' said a little voice. 'I'll go. I'm so small that if anything happens, I'll never be missed. I'll go. I'll bring back a lighted twig.' The stork looked down and there was the wren, fluttering about with her little head on one side and her wings quivering.

Although somewhat taken aback at this noble offer from so small a creature, the other birds were greatly relieved. They crowded around the little wren, giving her good advice. And when she asked someone to pluck her a twig, the pigeon said: 'Take two! Take two!' and put strong ones into her little beak.

Away flew the wren. Higher and higher and higher until she and her twigs were out of sight.

The other birds gathered together such sticks as they could find, prepared a bonfire and then waited anxiously. Time passed. The wren did not return. They looked at the sky, hoping that nothing had happened to her. She had been gone such a long time. Presently the hawk, with his keen sight, saw a little spark of fire, far off. It came nearer and nearer. 'She's coming,' cried the hawk, and before long down flew the wren with the burning twigs in her beak. She dropped them on to the bonfire, which burst into flames. Then the snow began to melt and little by little the birds grew warm and happy.

At least – all save one! Down on the ground the little

wren lay shivering and naked. She had been so close to the sun that all her feathers had been burnt. The poor little soul was quite bald.

When the other birds saw the little creature who had sacrificed so much, they were ashamed of their selfishness. 'Wren!' they cried. 'Wren darling, never mind! We'll look after you! No one shall ever tease you for having no feathers. Never mind!'

But the little wren only lay there shivering and crying, 'My feathers! I want my feathers!'

'Cheer-up! Cheer-up! Cheer-up!' cried a voice, and there was the sparrow looking very pleased and perky. 'We'll each give you a feather, won't we, birds?'

'O sparrow,' cried the others, 'how clever of you to think of that! Of course we will. Come, little wren.'

They clustered round the tiny shivering creature and from their own downy feathered coats they plucked soft bits of fluff and small shiny plumes, until at last the brave little wren had a covering of down all over its body except for one wee spot where there was only room for the smallest extra feather.

The stork clapped his beak. 'One more, please,' he said. 'Somebody here has not given a feather. Who is it?'

Nobody answered and all the birds looked at one another in astonishment. Who *could* have refused to help the wren? Suddenly the cock looked up and crowed loudly. 'It's you-dle-oodle-oo!'

His voice was angry and he pointed his beak at the owl, who was trying to hide in a tree.

'Cheer-up! Cheer-up!' cried the sparrow. 'You'll never miss *one* feather.'

But the owl refused to come out of the tree and when the stork asked him why he would not give up a feather, he sulkily hooted: 'Too-few! Too-few!'

'If you have too few,' cried the sparrow, 'I will give another, but mind you never let me see you again.'

So the wren was given a complete covering and ever since that day has been honoured by all the birds. But because the owl would not help the brave little bird who fetched the fire, the others will have nothing to do with him, and so he is afraid to come into their sight, and only dares to come out at night.

If you listen after dark, you will probably hear him still making the same excuse: 'Too-few! Too-few!'

7 King Solomon's Umbrella

Once upon a time, there was a king called Solomon. He was so wise that he knew the language of all the birds, the beasts and the fish; he could talk with the sun, the moon and the stars, and he understood what the wind whispered when it came down from the hills. One day Solomon had to travel across the sandy desert to a palace in another land. The journey took many days and the gentlemen of the court came with him, and he had slaves to wait on him, and white donkeys and camels to carry his baggage.

At first the days passed pleasantly enough. As time went on, the heat grew greater. The animals toiled with their burdens, looking patient and tired. The gentlemen of the court walked beside Solomon, fanning him with long feather-fans and palm leaves. But still it grew hotter and hotter. Solomon had never known the rays of the sun to beat down so fiercely. At last, when everyone was almost fainting with the heat, Solomon looked up and spoke to the sun.

'Come, come, come, brother!' said he kindly. 'Surely you see that we are all suffering. Why not shine a little more gently, sun?'

The sun smiled a beaming hot smile and took no notice. The animals panted for breath and the slaves moaned. Solomon spoke again.

'Sun!' said he more severely. 'I have asked you to shine a little more gently. We are weary with the great heat and can hardly make our journey.'

But the sun only beamed down more fiercely than ever, and the courtiers were so hot that they hadn't the strength to go on fanning the king. Once again Solomon looked up at the sky.

'This is not kind, O my brother,' said he. 'I have asked you twice to shine more gently, and you have shone more fiercely than ever. Surely you can do me this little service?'

The face of the sun grew fiery red. He glared down at Solomon.

'Service!' he scolded, in a deep hot voice. 'Who is King Solomon that he thinks the sun is his servant? Your duty is to rule over your people. My duty is to shine as well as I can. I shall do my duty.'

The angry red face glowered and the heat became worse. But King Solomon was a wise man. He saw that the sun was in a bad temper and so he did the wisest thing possible. He stopped arguing. But how could he continue his journey? His slaves and courtiers and animals were all lying on the ground overcome with the heat.

Solomon was just wondering what to do when a little bird – a hoopoe – fluttered on to his shoulder and began to chirp.

'O king!' it twittered. 'Peace be with you! What a hot day! Your nose is getting sunburnt; let me shelter it.'

The hoopoe flew above the king's nose and kept the sun off it with his wings. Solomon was highly amused.

He looked at the excited little bird with a twinkle in his eye.

'Well done, little brother!' said he. 'My nose was beginning to feel quite sore. If only you were bigger, you could shelter us all. The sun refuses to shine gently.'

The hoopoe twittered angrily.

'O king! I have never seen such a sulky red face in all my life. Making you too hot, is he? *I'll* see about it, I will.'

It gave the king a polite peck on the top of the head and flew off. Solomon laughed, but because he was wise, he knew that the hoopoe really wanted to help, so he sat down and waited.

After a while he noticed in the distance something which looked like a small black cloud. Nearer it came, and nearer, until at last Solomon saw that it was not a cloud but a flock of birds, flying so closely together that they looked like a black cloud in the sky. They were all hoopoes, and they were led by the little creature which had been so angry with the sun.

Gasping a little for breath, the leader fluttered above Solomon's head.

'O king,' it twittered; 'I have brought the whole family. Here are my grandparents and my father and my mother and my wife and my children and my brothers and my sisters and my uncles and my aunts and my cousins and all their families!'

It paused for breath and Solomon smiled and greeted the birds: 'Good day, little brothers! Peace be with you, little sisters! What can I, King Solomon, do for you?'

When they heard this, the hoopoes looked greatly astonished. The voice of their leader was shocked.

'What can King Solomon do for *us*? O king, we have come to do something for *you*! We are going to fly closely together over your head and shield you and your friends from the sun. We are going to be your umbrella!'

Solomon was delighted. He stood up and called to his companions: 'Come, my friends, arise and make the journey. The sun cannot trouble us. We have an umbrella of birds.'

One by one the courtiers and the slaves rose and stood behind Solomon. Even the tired animals tossed their heads and began to look happier.

Once again they all set out. Hour after hour the sun shone fiercely, but he could do no harm to anyone, because all the hoopoes, flying close together, shaded the travellers.

At last the journey came to an end. The animals were led into their stables, the tired slaves and courtiers lay down to rest, and Solomon stood alone in the garden. He turned his back on the sun, which was sinking rather sulkily behind the hills, and he spoke softly: 'Little brother Hoopoe, where are you?'

'Here I am, O king,' answered the hoopoe.

Solomon stroked its feathers.

'You have helped me, little brother,' he said. 'It was a kind thought to bring your friends to make me an umbrella. What reward can I give you and the other hoopoes? You shall have whatever you like.'

The hoopoe could scarcely believe its ears. It fluttered and twittered, twittered and fluttered, and at last managed to speak a few words, with little gasps in between.

'O king! O King Solomon! Let me go and ask my friends.'

Away flew the hoopoe, and Solomon waited until it came back. He saw that it was doing its best to look calm, but its eyes were glowing and its feathers twitching.

'Well, little brother?'

'O king! My friends and I would like to look nobler than any other bird. Please give us each a golden crown – solid gold – that everyone will envy.'

Solomon sighed, and looked at the excited bird. 'Are you sure, little brother?' he asked sadly.

'Oh yes, king, quite sure.'

'So be it then. Go back to your homes. You shall have solid golden crowns. Good night, little brother.'

Solomon turned away and went into the palace. Next day when the light was just dawning, the hoopoes awoke with strangely heavy heads. They looked at one another, and then set up such a song of joy that the whole world echoed.

'We have golden crowns! We have golden crowns! Look at us! Look at us! We are kings and queens!'

Up in the air they rose with their golden crowns shining. All day they flew about the world singing:

'Look at our crowns, our golden crowns!'

Here, there, and everywhere they flew, and soon everyone knew that the hoopoes had solid golden crowns.

But, alas for the poor little birds! Out of the houses came men, women and children with bows and arrows, sticks and stones, nets and traps. Down shone the sun triumphantly, making the golden crowns glitter, and whenever the people saw something sparkle, they shouted 'Gold! Gold!' and came with their nets and their weapons.

The hoopoes flew into the darkest places, but the golden crowns glimmered and betrayed them. They sped away as fast as they could, but the arrows overtook them. They hid in the trees, but sticks and stones came crashing through the branches. They couldn't even alight on the ground without a trap going 'snap' or a net taking them prisoner. The hoopoes had golden crowns and everyone envied them. The poor little bird who had first thought of making Solomon an umbrella was in great distress. It flew hither and thither trying to find some place where it could hide its companions and get away from that envious cry of 'Gold! Gold!' At last, weary with fear, it fluttered helplessly into Solomon's garden, and dropped like a stone at the king's feet. Solomon stooped down and lifted it in his hand.

'Little brother!' he whispered, caressing its feathers. 'What is the matter, little brother!'

'O king', whispered the hoopoe, 'take back your gift. Everyone envies our golden crowns and we cannot rest.'

'Poor little brother,' said Solomon gently.

The hoopoe looked up at him piteously.

'We thought such riches would make us happy! But now we know that to be envied does not mean to be happy. We do not want golden crowns; we want nothing more than our feathers.'

'Go home, little brother,' said Solomon. 'Be contented and you will be happy.'

The next day the hoopoes found that all their golden crowns had disappeared. In their place, each had a little crown of tufted feathers.

And to this day the hoopoes in the Middle East have crowns of feathers to show how they once helped Solomon.

8   The Four Friends and the Hunter

Once upon a time there were three friends – as different as chalk from cheese. They did not even live in the same kind of house, for one was more at home in the air, the other in the water and the third under the ground. These three friends were a raven, a turtle and a rat! Different as they were, they were never tired of each other's company, and if any one of them was in a difficulty the others would move might and main, to help him out of it.

Now, of course, as the three friends had such different ways of living, they could not spend all their time together. The raven naturally spent most of his time flying about in the air or sitting on the tops of trees. It was a good life and he was able to see all sorts of things that the others knew nothing about. The turtle, too, had quite an interesting time in his way. He did not move about very much because he was rather slow and solid. But he was none the worse for that. I dare say you have found out for yourselves that very often the people who cannot run fast or jump high are quite interesting to talk to! Old sober-sides, the turtle, was like that. He moved slowly, but he thought deeply, and the others found him a most intelligent companion. The rat was rather different. He could not fly like the raven, but he could swim just as well as the turtle. He was a quick mover and a quick thinker. But he did not always reflect deeply. He was one of those people who jumped to sudden conclusions, but still, he was a man of action, and he was useful.

And so with the raven to bring news, the turtle to think things out and the rat as a man of action, the friendship was a very successful one.

Every evening the three would meet together and talk over the affairs of the day. One day when they were sitting together having a pleasant chat beside a deep pool of water, the raven suddenly shouted 'Look!' The others turned their heads. Running towards them was a little wild goat. Out of breath and untidy, she scurried along with her stumpy little tail bobbing about her and her thin little legs twinkling as quickly as the sails of a windmill in a storm.

'Huh! Huh! Huh!' gasped the little goat.

'Good gracious! How she runs!' croaked the raven. 'One might almost believe she had wings.'

The turtle poked his head out of his shell, swinging it from side to side like the pendulum of a clock. He cleared his throat. 'Ahem,' said he. Slowly and quietly came the words; 'The goat travels as though she had wings because she is flying from something. The goat is flying from something because she is afraid. The goat is afraid of nothing but the Hunter!'

'Ee! Ee! Ee! Save yourselves!' squeaked the rat, and darted into a hole. The raven followed his example and flew to the top of a tree, where he could see the Hunter a long way off. As for the turtle, he crawled to the edge of the pool and flopped under the water.

The three friends were completely hidden when the little goat came panting up to the pool of water. She stood still, trembling, and her tail bobbed quickly from side to side. She cast a frightened look behind her, then stooped to the water for a drink. But the pool had been slightly ruffled by the turtle's plunge and she was afraid.

At this moment the raven, who had been looking over the hills, croaked out: 'It's all right. You can all come out. The Hunter has gone back.' And up to the surface of the water came the turtle, blinking at the little goat in a kindly way.

'Come along. Come along,' said he. 'You needn't be afraid now. You're quite safe. Drink as much as you like.'

'Yes, to be sure!' said the rat, scrambling out of his hole and sitting on his hind legs so as to clean his whiskers with his forepaws. 'Drink as much as you like. Stay here as long as you like.'

The goat began to drink. The raven flew down from the tree to a low shrub, and the turtle swam slowly out of the pool and began to think. He looked around with his bright eyes, and his queer little flat-topped head moved slowly from side to side. 'One alone is lonely,' said he. 'Two together may quarrel. So far three is a good partnership, but there's safety in numbers. What do you say, raven?'

'I say, "Yes",' croaked the raven and flew down and settled on the goat's back.

'And I,' said the rat, 'say, "Certainly. Why not?" Of course, the more the merrier.'

And he stopped cleaning his whiskers and gave a flip with his tail so that it coiled three times round the goat's left foreleg.

And that was how the little wild goat was taken into partnership. She gladly promised to remain with the three friends, because, as the turtle said, 'One alone is lonely' and 'There's safety in numbers'. Until she joined the three friends, the little goat had always been lonely or frightened, and now she had the raven to warn her of trouble that was coming, the turtle to give her good advice and the rat to encourage her to be brave.

At first she never ventured very far from the pool, for if the rat happened to be away, the turtle was sure to be there, and the little goat had had such a fright in the past that she never felt safe unless she knew that a friend was near. She dared not venture farther afield. The raven tried to tempt her with stories of green hills and juicy leaves. The old turtle gave her advice, telling her that nobody ought to be entirely dependent on friends; everybody must learn to stand on his own two feet. 'You see, Nanny,' said he to the goat, 'if *we* couldn't stand on our own feet and do things without help, *we* couldn't do anything for you! We are all dependent on one another, but no one can depend on a person who can't depend on himself.'

'Ma-a,' said the poor little goat, sadly. She knew it was true, and even when the rat tried to encourage her by squeaking 'Eek!' and scuttling off, she was afraid to follow. It took the little creature a very long time to get over her timidity.

But the time passed and she really did begin. She started to run after the rat, playfully butting him with her horns, and when he hid in the grass and allowed her to pass without seeing him, she actually went as far as the green hill and tasted the juicy leaves which the raven had described.

Never had she tasted such a good meal in her life, and what's more, she didn't feel in the least afraid. After that she went off by herself every day and returned to the pool in the evening to talk with her three friends.

For several weeks all went well. Every morning the four friends went about their own business, and every evening they met at the water's edge and talked over their various doings. Then one evening the goat did not come home. They waited, trying to pretend that nothing had happened, but as the evening wore on, each face began to look very anxious. At last the turtle broke the silence. 'I believe,' said he, solemnly waving his head from side to side, 'I believe if one wants to find what is lost the best thing to do is to look for it.'

'Ee, ee, ee!' said the rat, and was about to dart off when the turtle called him back, for the raven had already mounted in the air and was flying high above the trees. Wheeling in wide circles, he looked about him and presently flew down, clapping his beak nervously and flapping his wings, 'Alack! Alack!' he croaked. 'She's caught on the hill in the Hunter's net. What shall we do?'

The turtle, who had been thinking in his shell, suddenly popped out his head and spoke. 'When danger is at hand one should lose no time!' said he. 'One should likewise make use of one's resources.'

'Ee!' squeaked the rat. 'Stop croaking, Raven. Turtle's right as usual. We must use our resources. Carry me to Nanny, and I'll gnaw the net.'

Without a moment's delay, the raven caught the rat up in its beak and flew with all speed to the prisoner.

The goat was in a pitiful condition, but her face brightened as soon as she saw her friends, and when the rat had gnawed through the meshes of the net, she shook herself free and began to skip and jump for joy. But alas! her joy soon turned to horror, for what could she see coming up the hill but two figures. One was quite near, coming slowly, and the other neither near nor far, but coming quickly. The first was the turtle and the second was the Hunter.

'Ma-a-a!' cried the goat in distress. 'Oh, Turtle! Ma-a-a! Why did you come? I can run away, the raven can fly into the trees, and the rat can dart into a hole. But you, dear old slow-of-foot, you'll get caught. Ma-a-a! Ma-a-a! Why did you come?'

At this moment the rat squeaked 'Ee!' and darted into a hole. The raven flew to the top of a high tree, and the Hunter came up. The goat had just time to escape and hide behind a bush, but the turtle could not cover the ground quickly enough. In the twinkling of an eye the Hunter, furious at finding nothing in his net, seized the turtle and bundled him into a sack. 'Anyhow,' said he, 'if I can't have roast goat, I'll have turtle soup,' and slinging the bag over his shoulder, he turned and went down the hill.

The three friends came from their hiding-places. The raven was croaking with anxiety and the rat squeaking with distress. Strangely enough, the goat seemed to be the only person who kept her head.

'Ma-a-a! Ma-a-a!' said she. 'I'll pretend to be lame. The Hunter will drop his bag and run after me. Then rat can gnaw the rope, raven can peck open the bag and turtle can creep home.'

Without waiting for a reply, she ran off. For the first time in her life she was depending on herself, and the others trusted her. Taking a short cut round some bushes, she suddenly appeared before the Hunter, limping and bleating. The Hunter threw down his bag and began to chase her. The goat ran on, rather fast, stopping every now and then to limp and to bleat. On and on she led the Hunter, now here, now there, and so cleverly did she manage that at last he gave up the chase and returned to pick up his bag.

He did not see the bright eyes of a bird watching him from a high tree. He did not see the bright eyes of a rat peering at him from a little hole. He did not notice that the water in a pool was ruffled and muddy as though something had flopped into it rather quickly. All he found was an empty bag and a piece of frayed rope. Angrily he kicked the bag and stumped down the hill.

'I'll catch that goat yet,' he said.

But he never did.

When he was out of sight, back came the four friends to the pool on the other side of the hill. The raven croaked contentedly; the rat squeaked with joy; the little goat capered up and down saying, 'Ma-a-a! Ma-a-a!' As for the old turtle, he went on wagging his head. 'Yes, yes,' said he. 'We're all dependent on one another. But no one can depend on the person who can't depend on himself.'

9 Peter and Brother Robin

Once upon a time there lived three good old men whose names were Benedict, Bernard and Peter. They were monks, and poor ignorant people used to sit at their feet listening while they told stories of Jesus Christ.

Benedict, Bernard and Peter lived in Ireland. Each had a separate little house made of stones piled one on top of the other and stuck together by mud. There were no windows in the little houses, only a door, and the floor had no carpet or mat. It wasn't even made of wood. It was just the bare earth. There were no tables or chairs. The old monks used to sit on big round stones or logs of wood, and when they wanted to sleep they used to lie on the ground with a lump of wood instead of a pillow.

They were very poor, but they did not mind because they

had so many good friends. The people who listened to their stories used to bring them little presents. Sometimes it would be a piece of fresh butter wrapped up in a dock-leaf, sometimes a new round cheese or a loaf of bread, sometimes a bottle of milk.

Everyone loved the three kind old men. Even the birds and the animals used to have a friendly word with them. When Benedict went through the woods to pick wild strawberries he was sure to meet a rabbit or a hare, who would stop and nibble something at his feet and bob a friendly tail at him.

And when Bernard passed along the meadows on his way to visit some poor sick woman, he would stoop down to smell the flowers, and the bees would all begin to buzz round his head, getting quite excited and saying: 'Here'zzz Bernard! Here'zzz Bernard!'

But Peter was the one the birds liked. He couldn't step outside his little stone hut without the most extraordinary commotion in the sky. As soon as they saw him all the birds would come flying down to greet him, twittering and chirruping. He had only to hold up a finger, and two or three would come and perch on his hand. They would settle on his shoulder and on his head and if he sat down they would even come and hop about on his lap.

Peter was very fond of them all, especially the robin. Bernard and Benedict used to tease him, because he never went to sleep without poking his head round the side of the door saying: 'Good night, Brother Robin.' The robin always answered, and it even used to wake Peter in the morning by singing a song outside his door. Bernard and Benedict used to laugh and say: 'I don't believe Peter would ever get up in the morning if it weren't for little Brother Robin.'

But there came a day when they never laughed at Peter and his robin again, a day when they were only too glad to find that the robin loved Peter.

It happened like this.

One day Benedict, Bernard and Peter decided to sail away from Ireland and carry the gospel of Jesus Christ across the sea to Brittany. They knew that the people who lived there had never heard of Jesus, and they thought: 'The teaching of Jesus has brought us peace and hope and love. We mustn't keep it to ourselves. We must share it with others. We'll go across the sea and tell these people all about it.'

You can imagine how busy they were after that. It took them a long time to make a boat and to collect provisions, and of course it took them a long time to say good-bye to all their friends.

Poor Benedict could hardly bear to go through the woods; he felt so sad when he knew that he must leave the friendly little rabbits and hares. Bernard sighed deeply when the bees came buzzing round his head. He wondered whether he would ever see them again.

But Peter was the saddest of all, and he took so long to say good-bye to the robin that the others were almost angry with him and said:

'It will be very good for you to be without Robin. He makes you waste a lot of time. Get into the boat now, and come along.'

So Peter took up the oars and, seating himself behind Benedict and Bernard, began to row. Presently, they hoisted a sail and the wind blew them faster and faster from the coast of Ireland, until there seemed to be nothing but the grey water all round them and the grey sky all above them.

For five days they were at sea, and then at last they found themselves before a rocky coast. Very carefully they steered their boat to the shore, pulled it inland and began to look around.

At first it all seemed very strange and unfriendly, but when the monks had wandered round a little, they found a pleasant spot near a little wood with green hills stretching away into the distance, and a big cave which gave them a ready-made home.

The three old men were delighted. Of course the first thing Benedict did was to go into the woods; and immediately three rabbits popped up, sat back on their haunches, bobbed their tails and flopped their ears as much as to say: 'Good morning, Benedict, here we are again.' And Benedict felt quite at home.

'Come to us-zz! He's-zz come to us-zz!' hummed the bees when Bernard climbed the hill looking for flowers. And, of course, Bernard felt quite at home, too.

Only Peter was homesick. All the birds greeted him cheerily, but he could not find one Brother Robin. He was so sad and silent that, old as he was, Benedict began to scold him, just as though he were a naughty child instead of an old grey-haired monk with a wrinkled face.

'Now look here, Peter,' he said, 'Brother Robin always prevented you from doing your work and made you waste time. You ought to be very thankful that he's not here. So stop looking miserable and go about your work cheerfully. None of the poor people here know anything about Jesus. We must build them a church and teach them to come and say their prayers.'

Peter tried to smile, but his heart was very heavy. Before he went to rest in the cave at night, he used to stand just outside and wait, but Brother Robin wasn't there to chirp 'Good night', and no little voice sang a song to wake him in the morning.

However, he worked hard and soon the others began to think that he had forgotten all about Brother Robin. They never mentioned the little bird. They talked about their work, about the people who were beginning to listen to their stories and to learn prayers to say in the church which the old men had built of wood.

They sometimes talked about food, because they lived upon wild fruit, and berries and mushrooms, and roots which they boiled to make soft. They wished they could have some bread, but the people weren't yet friendly enough to give them presents, and they had forgotten to bring any grain with them in their boat, so they could not sow any corn.

After a time the poor old monks began to feel the want of bread. They looked very thin and hungry.

At last Peter, who was the oldest and the weakest, fell ill. The others did their best for him, but he seemed to grow worse and worse. Every day Bernard and Benedict knelt beside him and fed him with berries, soft roots and herbs, but he seemed to have lost hope. He could only say: 'I should die happy if I thought that you two old friends could have bread.'

Day after day the poor old man grew weaker, and the others were in great distress. One day they carried him out of the cave and put him under the shade of a tree where he could watch the sun set. But he took no interest. He lay with half-closed eyes, whispering over and over again: 'Give us this day our daily bread.' Suddenly he opened his eyes and seemed to listen.

'Brother Robin,' he whispered eagerly and his face grew bright.

The others looked around in astonishment. They could see nothing. Peter struggled to his knees and stretched out his hands. 'Brother Robin,' he cried. And down fluttered a little redbreast! It looked at Peter out of its bright eyes, put its head first on one side, then on the other, and then very gently dropped an ear of corn into Peter's hand. When Peter's hand had closed over the corn the robin perched on his foot, and sang and sang and sang.

As for Peter he bent his head and whispered: 'Praise the Lord, O my soul.'

From that minute he grew better, and in later times

neither he nor Benedict nor Bernard was ever hungry again, for they planted the ear of corn which Brother Robin had brought and, in the years which followed, their fields were full of grain.

10   The Goatherd and the Goats

It was a cold stormy day, and down the hillside came a goatherd driving his goats. Their backs were white with snow and the poor creatures huddled together, bleating pitifully.

'Beh-eh-eh,' said the billy goats. 'Beh-eh-eh. It's co-o-old!'

'Meh-eh-eh,' cried the nanny goats. 'Meh-eh-eh. It's we-et.'

And the little kids whimpered and shivered. 'Eh-eh-eh. It's free-ee-eezing! We want to get war-ar-arm, wa-ar-arm! Eh-eh-eh! Eh-eh-eh!'

And they all stood in a bunch together and didn't move.

By this time the snow was falling thick and fast and the goatherd himself was getting cold.

'Come, come, my little friends,' said he. 'This won't do. You can't stay out in the snow all night. You'll be frozen to death.'

But the goats only looked at him with their big brown eyes and said: 'Eh-eh-eh. Eh-eh-eh.'

Then the goatherd began to coax them. 'There's a cave half-way down the hill,' he said. 'You can shelter there. You shall have the cabbage stalks I've got for you here in my sack, and I'll pick some nice leaves for you from the shrubs. Come along!'

'Meh-eh-eh,' said the nanny goats. 'He's our ma-a-aster.'

And the kids bleated: 'A ca-a-ave! Hur-reh-eh-eh! Hur-eh-eh-eh!'

And with their little horns butting and their little tails bobbing and their little hooves crunching the snow, they ran helter-skelter down the hillside until they came to the cave.

Suddenly they stood still. The billy goats sniffed. The nanny goats sniffed. And little kids sniffed. 'Eh, eh-eh. Who's he-e-ere?'

'Hm,' said the goatherd. 'Surely I smell something! I do! I smell goat – *wild* goat.'

'We-'re ta-a-ame,' bleated his own herd. 'Take us i-i-n.'

But the goatherd took no notice. He was peering into the cave. There were marks of little hooves in the ground and away inside the cave he could see lots of bright eyes looking at him.

'Aha-ha!' said he to himself. 'A herd of wild goats! Fine big creatures, much handsomer than my own animals.'

Then he took the sack from his shoulder, put it on the

ground, and begun to take out the cabbage stalks and leaves.

His own goats began to bleat: 'Eh-eh-eh, eh-eh-eh, ca-a-bbages.'

But he pushed them out of the way.

'Stop that!' he shouted. 'You can wait till tomorrow,' and he threw all the sweet cabbage stalks into the cave and the wild goats began to nibble them and to gobble them up. And while his own goats bleated pitifully, the goatherd began to strip leaves off the shrubs outside the cave and throw them in great handfuls to the wild goats inside.

'Now,' said he, 'they have plenty of food to last till the morning. When I come back tomorrow they'll still be here eating, and I'll be able to tie them up and take them home. Then I shall have two herds of goats, my own little ones and these fine big wild ones.'

'Beh-eh-eh,' said his own billy goats. 'It's co-c-old. Let us e-e-eat!'

'Me-eh-eh,' cried his own nanny goats. 'We're hu-u-ungry!'

While the little kids bleated 'Eh-eh-eh' and shivered beside the cave, the wild goats ate the cabbage stalks – crunch, crunch, crunch. Then the goatherd put some branches in front of the cave to shut the hole. 'There,' he said, 'that will stop them from getting out. Now, you others, you can shelter under the tree. I'll be back in the morning.' And away he went down the hillside to his cottage and banged at the door.

'Let me in, good wife!' said he.

'You're welcome home, good man,' said she.

'I'm cold. Is there cabbage soup?' asked he.

'It's ready, steaming hot,' said she.

And she ladled out of the saucepan some delicious hot cabbage soup.

'What kind of day have you had?' asked she.

'Very good. I went to the cave. I found some goats, good wife,' said he.

'But you've got some goats, good man,' said she.

'And I've found some more, good wife,' said he, 'very fine, very big, very sleek. I'll go up tomorrow and bring them home. And we'll be richer than our neighbours, for we shall have two herds and they've only one.'

That night the goatherd and his wife sat up late talking of what they would do when they were richer than anyone else in the village.

The next morning it had stopped snowing and they climbed the hill together. The wife carried a bag of cabbage leaves and the goatherd had a reed pipe, and he played the tune he always played when he wanted to call his goats.

'Funny,' said his wife. 'The goats don't answer.'

'Strange,' said he. 'The goats don't come.' And he played something gayer and quicker.

But still his own goats neither answered nor came, and at last the goatherd and his wife reached the mouth of the cave.

The goatherd stood still. His wife pulled his sleeve.

'What's the matter, good man?' asked she. 'You're as white as a sheet, good man. How now?

'The wild goats! They've gone, good wife,' cried he. 'They've pushed down the branches and all run away. See their tracks in the snow. Alas!'

'Do you mean to tell me, good man,' said she angrily, 'that we're just as poor as we were before?'

'We're – we're – p-poorer than ever. Alackaday! Good wife, look under the tree.'

Covered with last night's snow his own goats lay under the tree. While the wild goats were off and away to the woods, his own had died of hunger.

And that's the end of the story. You know what it means, don't you? Never neglect your old friends for the sake of new ones who may be more useful. If you do, you may lose them both.

11 Why the Lapwing has a Forked Tail

This is a story which comes all the way from Sweden, where the children love to gather round the fire and listen to stories which their grandmothers and great-grandmothers used to hear when they too were children. Many of the stories, like this one, are about the Holy Family.

Long ago, say the Swedes, Mary, the mother of Jesus, lived in a little wooden house on the hillside. She was always very busy, because Joseph, her husband, was only a poor carpenter, and so Mary had to do all the work of the house herself, look after her little boy, Jesus, and sometimes give Joseph a helping hand.

One day Joseph said to Mary:

'I mustn't disappoint my master, and yet I don't see how I can do all this work unless you spend more time helping me. Let little Jesus play by himself, and give some of your time to me.'

But Mary shook her head. 'I can't do that, Joseph,' she said. 'Our baby is still very little. He needs someone to care for him and watch over him. He is such a beautiful child that I'm afraid to leave him alone, lest someone should carry him away.' And she kissed Joseph, but she went back to little Jesus.

The days passed, and still Joseph had more and more work. Mary helped him in the evenings when her baby was asleep, but that was not enough, and he began to look so tired and old that at last she said: 'Dear Joseph, now that you have so much work, we are no longer very poor. Let us have a serving-maid to help in the house and to watch over little Jesus when he is asleep and then I can work with you in the carpenter's shop.'

When Joseph heard this, he was very glad and went into the village to find a young girl who would come to Mary as serving-maid. From house to house he went, but somehow or other everyone made an excuse. It was: 'Oh no, Joseph. Our daughter is wanted at home'; or, 'I'm sorry, Joseph, but our daughter has just found a place – she's with some very rich people in the next village'; or, 'Oh no, Joseph. You live too far away. We can't send our daughter to a house on the hill.'

Poor Joseph began to grow discouraged. He went from house to house without any success, until he came to the last cottage in the village. He knocked at the door. There was no answer. He knocked again, and after a few minutes a woman came to the door. Her eyes were wet and her apron was crumpled. She looked as though she had been crying very bitterly.

Joseph was sorry for her. 'I'm afraid you're unhappy,' he said. 'Forgive me for disturbing you, but I'm looking for a little servant-girl who will come to my house on the hill and help to do the work.'

When the woman heard this, she burst into tears and, leading the way into the house, pointed to a young girl who was standing by the table looking very sulky and miserable. 'Ah, Joseph,' said the woman. 'That's my daughter. I never thought I should live to be ashamed of my own daughter.'

Kind-hearted Joseph patted the girl on the shoulder. 'Is this the daughter you're ashamed of?' he asked. 'Well, well, I'm sure if she's done anything wrong, she's sorry. What's the matter?'

'The matter?' said the woman, still crying. 'Everything's the matter. She used to be a servant at one of the big houses, but they've turned her away. She has been stealing. My Helga's a thief!'

Joseph turned to the young girl. 'Are you really a thief, Helga?' he asked.

The girl hung her head and whispered: 'Yes, I did steal. And now nobody will give me work.' Two large tears rolled down her cheeks, but Joseph smiled at her.

'It is very wrong to take anything that doesn't belong to you,' he said 'but people can always conquer their faults if they try hard enough. Will you try not to steal if I take you back with me to be Mary's serving-maid?'

Helga nodded her head and Joseph looked at her very kindly. 'Very well,' he said. 'Dry your eyes and come back with me to the house on the hill. I know Mary will find you a great help.'

Helga dried her eyes, said good-bye to her mother, and away she went with Joseph, happy that she had been given another chance. When they arrived at the house, Mary came to meet them with the little Jesus in her arms. She was delighted to hear that Joseph had found a serving-maid and she soon showed Helga all her duties.

After Helga had been in the house for a few days, she knew that she was going to be very happy and comfortable. She learned how to look after the house, how to cook and how to sew; and when Mary was busy in the carpenter's shop, helping Joseph with his work, Helga used to take her needlework out of doors and sit on the step while the little baby Jesus slept in his cradle beside her.

Time passed very happily, until one day Helga lost her scissors. She had been sewing out of doors and she had looked for them everywhere, but she could not find them. At last, she went into the house, saying, 'Oh dear! I shall have to buy myself another pair.' Then suddenly she thought: 'Why, of course, Mary must have some scissors. I'll borrow hers, and put them back again afterwards.'

She went up to Mary's work-basket and took out the scissors. When she saw them, her eyes gleamed. They were so pretty.

'Why,' thought Helga, 'these must be very valuable.

They have gold handles.' She polished them a little with the corner of her apron and they shone still more. Helga looked at them with longing. 'Oh, I do wish they belonged to me,' she said.

She looked at them again and began to wonder what she would do if the little gold-handled scissors belonged to her. 'I'd sell them,' she thought. 'Yes, I'd take them into the village and I'd go to the goldsmith and ask him to melt down the handles and give me some money for the gold, and then I'd buy some feathers to put in my hat and a new grey dress.'

She looked at the scissors again and suddenly she thought, 'Mary will never know. She hardly ever sews. She doesn't really want them and I *do* so need a new grey dress and some feathers for my hat.' And Helga, forgetting all about the promise which she had made to Joseph, took the scissors and hid them in her mattress. The next day she sold them in the village and came home with the money, meaning to buy herself a new grey dress and some feathers as soon as she had a holiday.

But the money was of no use to Helga. That evening Mary wanted to sew. She found her thimble and she found her needles, but she could not find her scissors. She hunted high and low, and Helga, looking very much ashamed and unhappy, hunted with her. But the scissors were nowhere to be seen, and Mary was very much distressed. Just as she was beginning to give up the search, there was a knock at the door.

'Come in,' said Mary.

The door opened and in walked the goldsmith.

Helga grew pale with fear, for he had in his hand a pair of gold scissors. She began to cry.

'Are those my scissors, Helga?' asked Mary, and her voice was sorrowful.

Helga looked at the ground and shuffled her feet. 'Yes,' she whispered.

Mary looked at her very sadly, but the goldsmith was angry.

'I knew she was a thief,' he cried, 'and now she shall go before the judges and be punished.' He took her by the hand opened the door, while Helga wept: 'Let me go! Let me go! I only wanted feathers for my hat and a new grey dress.'

But the goldsmith would not listen. Then a strange thing happened. Mary ran to the door and put her arms round Helga's neck. 'My child,' she said, 'you shall go free. You shall have feathers for your head and a grey dress. But listen, I cannot save you from all your punishment. Take my scissors and always carry them with you to remind you never to steal again.'

As she spoke, there was a strange cry. Helga slipped from the goldsmith's grasp and began to change. A tuft of feathers grew out of her head, grey and white feathers covered her body. She became smaller and smaller. Suddenly she rose in the air on two wings and flew round the house crying:

'A-ah-me! A-ah me!'

The goldsmith rubbed his eyes, but all he could see was a grey and white bird with a forked tail like a pair of open scissors.

The Swedes say that the lapwing or pee-wit always carries a tail like a pair of open scissors to remind it of the time when it was once a little serving-maid who stole Mary's scissors.

If you see one, listen and you will hear it crying sadly: 'A-ah me! A-ah me!'

12　Ching, Chang, and the Nugget

Once upon a time there were two friends who lived in China. One was called Chang and the other Ching. Each wore a large round straw hat, a blue cotton coat and no shoes, but Chang had a yellow necklace made of amber beads, and Ching a green one made of soapstone.

The two boys had to work hard for their living, and so they did not have many holidays, but they spent all their spare moments together, and no one had ever seen them speak crossly to one another or look angry. When work was finished in the big factory where they stood all day weaving silk, Chang and Ching would carry their bowls of rice into the shade of some tree, take out their chop-sticks and eat together. If one had more rice than the other, he shared it with his friend. Ching took the greatest delight in Chang's company, and Chang was never so happy as when he was with Ching.

One day when the sky was very blue and even the dusty city smelt of sunshine, the owner of the factory was married. Because it was his wedding day and he wanted everyone to feel happy, he gave his workers a holiday. 'You shall each have a penny to spend,' said he.

The workers were delighted. One after another they went up to receive their pennies, but Chang and Ching came hand in hand. They were the last, and there was only one penny left. The master was troubled. His face grew red and he pushed his fingers into the corners of his big purse, but, search as he would, he could only find one penny.

Then the other workers began to laugh, but Chang and Ching knelt before their master and touched the ground with their foreheads. 'Honourable Master,' they said, 'do not distress yourself. Give the penny to Chang or to Ching, for what belongs to Chang belongs to Ching, and what belongs to Ching belongs to Chang. We are such good friends that we might be one person. You are keeping your promise. You have said "One penny to one person." '

The boys rose from their knees. Ching stretched out his hand and Chang put his on the top of it, and into the out-stretched palm the master dropped a penny.

Smiling with delight at their good fortune, the two boys wandered arm in arm out of the city into the country. The sun was shining so brightly that all the hills looked golden, and as the two friends passed along the sandy tracks a gentle breeze blew through the blossoming pear trees, and a host of pink and white petals fluttered like fairies around them, sometimes alighting on their broad-brimmed hats, sometimes dropping to the ground and lightly caressing their bare feet.

Chang and Ching wandered about, so happy in each other's company that they had no need to speak. At last they came to an old pine forest. The moss on the ground looked so soft and cool, and the deep green of the trees was so pleasantly shady that Chang and Ching left the hillside and strolled into the forest. Long streaks of shadow stretched across the ground, but the sun peeped through the branches and made the earth look as though it were caught in a golden net.

Suddenly the two boys stopped, and with one accord pointed to a little lump of brightness, no larger than a pine cone. It was lying on some moss near the root of a tree and its light was so dazzling that they rubbed their eyes.

Each asked the other, 'What is that?' and stooped to look at it.

'Ching,' said Chang, 'It's a nugget, a lump of pure gold. Dear friend, how glad I am of your luck. It's yours. You saw it first.' And he picked up the golden stone and put it into Ching's hand.

But Ching began to laugh. 'Why, Chang,' he said, 'We have always shared everything, our wages, our dinners, our holidays. These are little things of little value, but the nugget is a big thing and worth much. I have always longed for you to be rich, and now my wish will come true. Take the nugget. It is yours.'

'I, too, have longed for *you* to be rich,' said Ching, 'and now this nugget will bring you the wealth that I have always wanted for you. Keep it, Chang. It is yours.'

Chang's face flushed. 'I shall not keep it. Take it yourself,' he said.

Ching grew hot. The tiniest shadow of a frown appeared between his eyes. 'I won't,' he said. 'It's yours.'

Chang stamped his foot and Ching tossed his head. Suddenly they looked at each other in horrified amazement. For the first time in their lives they had begun to quarrel.

'Oh, Chang,' said Ching. He stooped and gently put back the nugget where he had found it.

Then, looking happily at the penny which they had been given by their master, the two friends put their arms around one another and strolled farther into the forest. They felt just as though they had nearly lost one another.

As time passed, the shadows in the wood began to lengthen and the network of sunshine changed from gold to pink.

'Let us rest for a little while, before we go home,' said Chang. 'The evening is quiet and beautiful.'

As the two boys sat down under a pine tree, they heard the sound of footsteps, and a whining voice murmured: 'Kind sirs, kind sirs, have pity on a poor old man.'

They looked up, and before them stood an old man. His eyes were heavy and tired, his face wrinkled, and his back bent. He stretched out a trembling hand.

'Give me something to buy some supper,' he begged.

Chang and Ching looked at him sorrowfully. 'Alas! poor

old stranger,' said they, 'we have only one penny.'

'But stay,' cried Ching suddenly; 'there is gold in the forest! Over there,' and he pointed in the direction in which he and Chang had been walking. 'There is a nugget as large as a pine cone.'

'Yes, indeed,' said Chang. 'Go and find it, old man, and you will grow rich.'

The beggar's eyes sparkled, and mumbling a word of thanks he shuffled off through the forest eagerly looking for the nugget.

Chang and Ching remained where they were. They talked about their penny, deciding what they would buy for supper when they returned to the town. They were enjoying themselves quietly when they were suddenly disturbed by an angry shout, and stumbling towards them came the old beggar, shaking his fist.

'Ah, you bad boys,' he cried, 'why did you not tell me the truth? What do you mean by sending me into the forest, looking for something which wasn't there? It was cruel of you to disappoint a poor, hungry old man.'

'My friend,' said Chang, 'we spoke the truth. We left the nugget lying by the root of a tree.'

'We did not mean to disappoint you,' said Ching. 'The nugget was there only a few minutes ago.'

'Nugget, indeed!' snorted the old beggar. 'There was an old apple, yellow with age. I picked it up and cut it in two because I was hungry. But even then I had to throw both halves away. There was a worm in the middle. You're cruel wicked boys to treat a poor beggar so.'

'Dear friend,' said Ching, 'you are making a mistake. Let us give him our penny, Chang. He is hungrier than we are.'

'Take the penny, old man. You are welcome to it,' said Chang, and he handed the coin to the beggar, who seized it with delight and hurried away, fearing that the two friends would change their minds.

When he had gone, Chang and Ching looked at one another. 'No supper for us,' they laughed. 'Let's go home,' and hand in hand they strolled back over the carpet of moss.

'How strange that he didn't find the nugget,' said Chang.

'Yes,' said Ching. 'It was there that we left it.'

They both looked down. For a minute they gasped with astonishment. Then, with a shout of delight, each ran forward and stooped to the ground. Two nuggets lay, golden and glittering, near the root of the old pine tree.

Chang picked up one and Ching the other.

Their faces were wreathed in smiles. With a little cry of joy Chang handed his nugget to Ching and Ching handed his to Chang. 'Dear friend,' said each boy with one voice, 'at last I am able to give you a real present.'

In the same series:

Seven Minute Tales

Rhoda Power

The stories in this delightful collection come from all parts of the world. 'Mimosa and the Wooden Bowl' is familiar to boys and girls in Japan, whilst children in Africa will tell you 'Why the Hippopotamus Took to the Water'. There are stories from many parts of Europe and from America too, all of them chosen and retold for your enjoyment.

My History of Music

Irene Gass

This book takes you on a musical journey through the ages. You can read about the early growth of music, the instruments which were the forerunners of our present-day brass, woodwind and strings, and about the time when daily music-making in all homes was the custom.

You will come across many famous composers from different countries on this musical journey. And, finally, Irene Gass suggests how each one of you can become a musical 'explorer' finding out more and more interesting things to add to this fascinating story of music.

Worzel Gummidge and
the Railway Scarecrows

Barbara Euphan Todd

This story mainly concerns Mildew Turmut, who
is Worzel Gummidge's sister and really rather grand –
she scares trains!

When a small boy called Robin comes to Scatterbrook
and makes friends with the scarecrows, strange things start
to happen. There is the singing cow, for example, and the
mystery train, not forgetting the Zoo which wasn't
quite a Zoo – because the animals wouldn't stay put.

Worzel Gummidge and the Treasure Ship

Barbara Euphan Todd

Robin and Marlene are very willing to help Miss Dollit open 'The Treasure Ship' but somehow the scarecrows become involved too, with rather odd results. Worzel Gummidge is given a job as a hatstand, Earthy Mangold is often to be seen drinking tea to encourage passers-by to join her. It is all very curious – especially when Saucy Nancy comes to adorn the tea-garden and Worzel Gummidge gives a lecture to a bird-watching club.

Come Follow Me

Poems for the very young

A lively and interesting collection of poems for
young children which has already delighted thousands
of readers all over the world.

The Zebra Book of Games and Puzzles

Carlton Wallace

Here for lively, inquiring minds are dozens of ideas, specially designed for parties and individual amusement. Included are matchstick puzzles, conundrums, magic, fun with balloons, the secrets of codes, charades, crosswords and many other exciting pastimes.

Two new Poetry Anthologies edited by Howard Sergeant:

Happy Landings

The Swinging Rainbow

Happy mixtures of old favourites and modern poems, these collections have been specially chosen to appeal to young children.